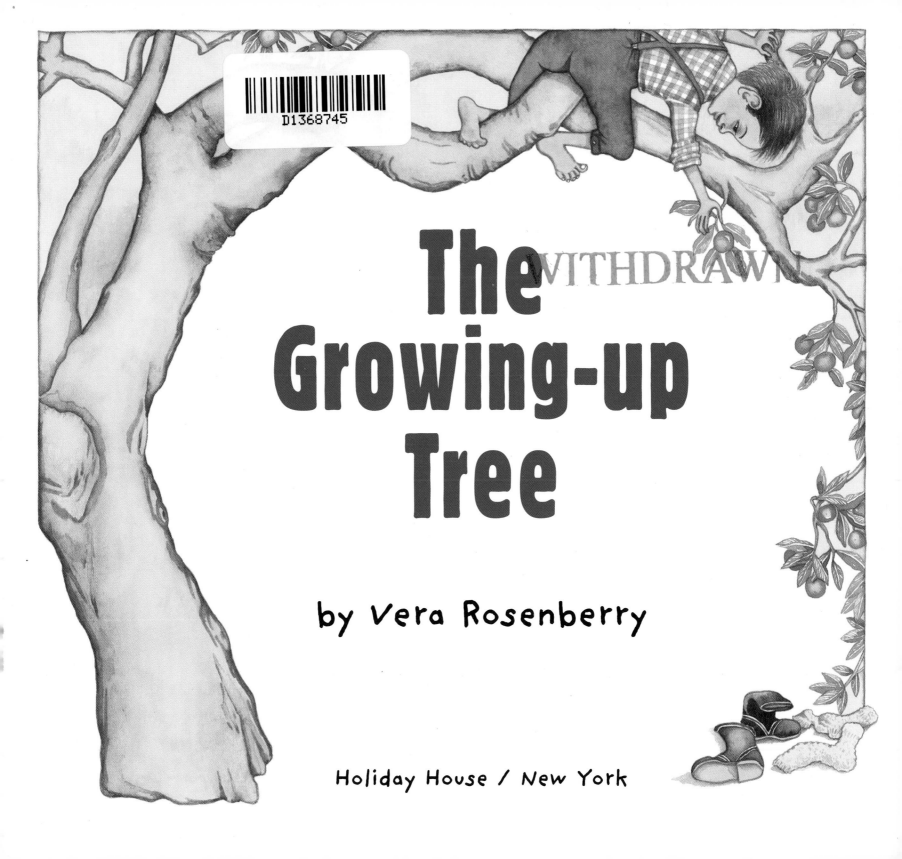

The Growing-up Tree

by Vera Rosenberry

Holiday House / New York

For Tanya,
who appreciates a great apple

Library of Congress Cataloging-in-Publication Data
Rosenberry, Vera.
The growing-up tree / Vera Rosenberry
p. cm.
Summary: The life of an apple tree,
planted by Alfred's mother when he was a baby,
parallels Alfred's life as he and his children
and grandchildren grow older together.
ISBN 0-8234-1718-2 (hardcover)
[1. Apples—Fiction. 2. Growth—Fiction.
3. Family—Fiction.] I. Title.
PZ7.R719154Gr 2003
[E]—dc21   2002191320

One day when Alfred was a tiny baby,
his mother rocked him in his cradle
out in the sunny garden.

She bit into an apple and said,
"This is the best apple I have ever tasted!"

She saved the seeds and planted
them right in that sunny corner.

One of the seeds sprouted
and began to grow.

"This will be Alfred's apple tree,"
said his mother.

When Alfred was one year old,
his baby apple tree was exactly his height.

By the time Alfred was five,
the tree produced its first apple.

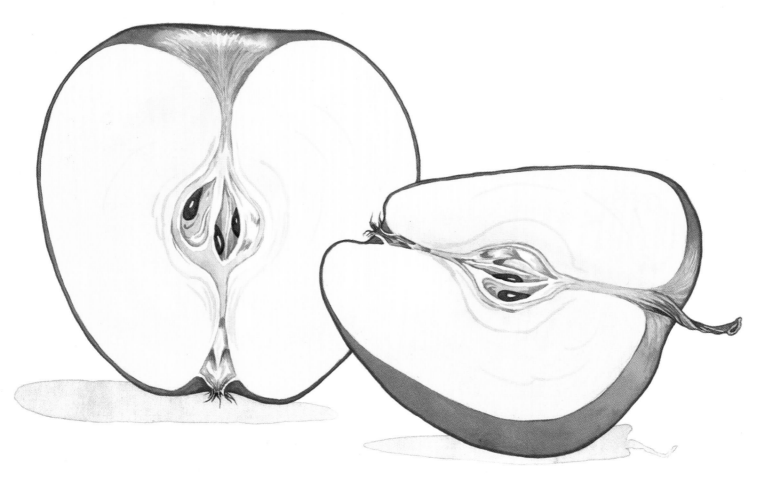

Alfred's mother carefully divided
the apple, and they each ate half.

"How delicious!" they agreed.

Alfred and the apple tree grew up together.
The apple tree gave Alfred shade

and beauty,

a place to climb

and sit,

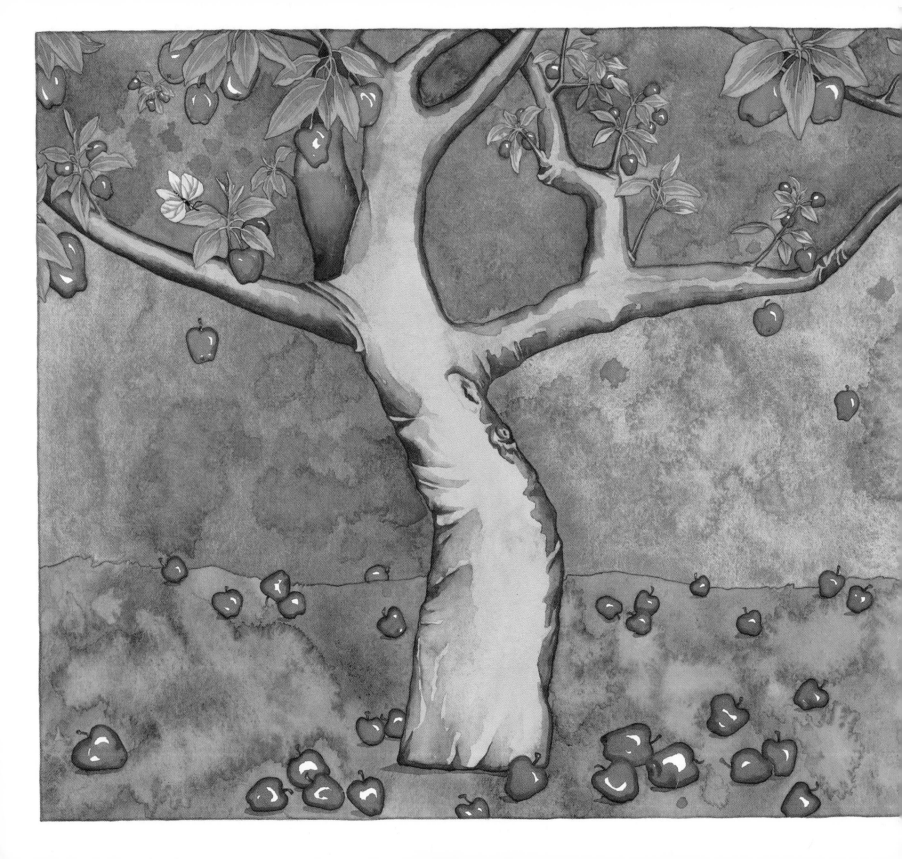

and many wonderful apples to eat.

Alfred gave the apple tree his love

and care.

Alfred married his sweetheart under fluttery drifts of fragrant pink and white apple blossoms.

His children grew up.

Later, their children grew up too.

Alfred sat under his apple tree
in its dappled shade.
Both of them were old and withered now.

One night there was a terrible storm.
Wind and rain lashed wildly against
the windows of the bedroom where
Alfred lay, his heart now still.

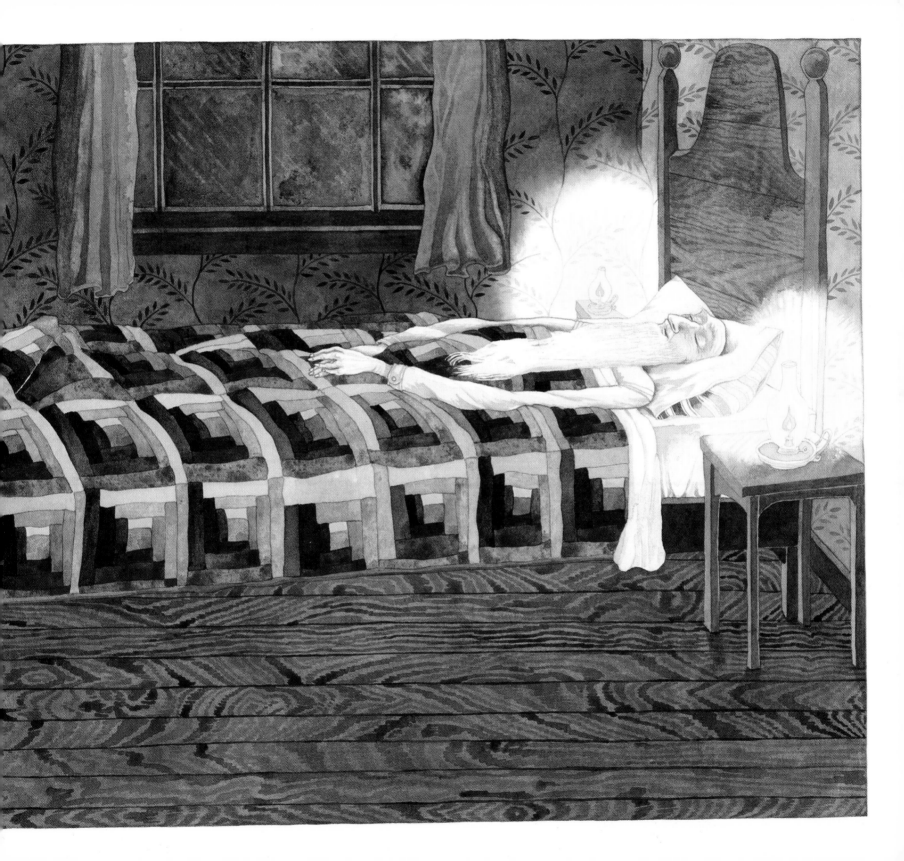

The next morning Alfred's apple tree
lay dead too, split open by the storm.

But an apple seed sprouted
in its place.

And it began
to grow.